by Marilyn D. Anderson

illustrated by Dennis E. Miller

cover illustration by Estella Lee Hickman

Published by Willowisp Press, Inc.
401 E. Wilson Bridge Road, Worthington, Ohio 43085

Originally published as *But Maggie Wanted a Pony*

Printed in the United States of America
10 9 8 7 6 5 4 3 2 1

ISBN 0-87406-262-4

1

"Maggie, see what Corky's barking about," Betty Johnson called over the whine of the vacuum cleaner.

Maggie Johnson, age 11, finished rearranging her stuffed animals and looked out the window. She saw a handsome gray station wagon in the driveway. "It's Tim and Jamie," she yelled on her way to the door.

Her mom shut off the vacuum at once and gathered up the cord. "Oh, my," she complained. "What will I give them for lunch?"

Her mother may have had mixed feelings about surprise guests, but Maggie didn't. She was delighted. Being the only child on a dairy farm was sometimes lonely, and even younger cousins were welcome playmates.

The small brown and white dog was jumping all over her cousins as Maggie reached them. "Corky, Corky, stop that," she ordered, but the dog paid no attention to her.

Tim stopped to pet the dog. "We don't mind. He's just glad to see us," he said.

"We like dogs," said his younger sister, Jamie.

"Well, hello, Andersons," called Mrs. Johnson from the front door. "What a surprise!"

"Hello, Betty," answered Maggie's Aunt Jane, catching up with her children. "Sorry we didn't warn you. We hadn't planned to come today. We just went for a drive, and here we are."

"Well, it's good to see you," said Maggie's mom as she hugged her sister.

"We've got a new archery set," said Tim to Maggie. "Let's set it up and have target practice."

Maggie hesitated. Tim always had something new to show her, and he delighted in playing teacher. It seemed she could never keep up with him.

"Oh, an archery set?" she asked, trying to sound enthusiastic. "When did you get that?"

"Mom bought it the day school was out," he

said. "She said she hoped it would keep us out of trouble for a while."

"Well, did it?" asked Maggie with a smile.

"Sort of, except for the hole I put in one of our lawn chairs trying to get an arrow out," Tim grinned.

"He already lost three of the arrows, too," said Jamie.

"Never mind, Tattletale," Tim warned. "Come on, Maggie. Let's see how good a shot you are."

Maggie wasn't a good shot at all. When she tried to hit the big straw-filled cushion, the arrow usually dropped just a few feet in front of her. It was hard to remember to let go of the bowstring and arrow at just the right time. Even when she got that part right, the arrow went too high or too low. After an hour of trying, she had only hit the target three times.

The Andersons had been practicing, and they were good shots. Tim had a high score, and even little Jamie did better than Maggie.

After lunch Tim wanted to climb trees. Maggie was a pretty good tree climber, but she never took crazy chances the way Tim did. He was Tarzan of the Apes one minute and a paratrooper the next. More than once she and Jamie held their breaths and waited to see if Tim would fall.

Later the three kids found some old skis in the garage which they promptly tried out on the grass. Mr. Johnson didn't appreciate that.

"Hey, you guys, does that look like snow to you?" he asked good naturedly. "Put those skis away. It's about time for Maggie to get the cows anyway. You can help her."

"Good deal," said Tim eagerly. "Where are

they? Do we need sticks to chase them?"

"They're in the pasture at the end of the lane," Maggie explained. "And you won't need sticks because the cows know it's milking time."

"Oh, now this sounds like work," he said, less enthusiastically.

"Let's pretend we're cowboys on a big cattle drive!" Maggie suggested. "I'll ride my black stallion, Thunder."

"Cowboys," he snorted. "Nobody plays cowboys anymore."

"But it's fun," she insisted. "Steady, Thunder. Easy, big fella," she told her own prancing feet.

"I'll ride my white stallion, Lightning," Jamie said eagerly. And her feet began to prance, too.

Tim groaned and said, "You two are crazy, but why not? I'll ride my palomino, Fireball. Race you to the cows!"

As they took off Maggie called, "Hey, we can't come running up on the cows like this. They'll head for the other end of the pasture. Slow down!"

Tim slowed "Fireball" and looked around. "What do you mean? I don't see any cows, yet. How far is it?" he asked.

"Well, it is quite a ways," Maggie admitted. "I just wanted you to know how to act when we get there."

"Do you round up the cows every night?" he wondered. "It seems like a lot of work."

Maggie nodded. "I don't mind, but it will be more fun when I get my pony," she hinted.

"Who says you're getting a pony?" Tim asked doubtfully.

"Dad," Maggie said. "He knows I want one. I must have asked him a million times."

"Did he say 'yes' for sure?" Jamie asked.

Maggie hesitated. "Well, he hasn't exactly said for sure," she admitted. "But he's been saying 'when you're older' for a long time now."

"Big deal," scoffed Tim. "My dad says things like that, too, when I'm not going to get something. Don't hold your breath."

The first open meadow was just ahead. They could see the herd of black and white cows scattered over it. They stopped so that Maggie could tell her cousins what to do. But first she had to make Tim understand. "I *am* going to get a pony," she told him. "And it will be soon. You'll see."

2

The following evening Maggie heard her parents arguing. They seemed to be talking about her. "You know she's been wanting a pony," her dad was saying.

"Well, I never thought you'd go out and spend so much money without discussing it with me," her mom answered angrily.

When they saw Maggie come into the room, they stopped talking immediately. "It's time for supper," Maggie's mom told her. "Please wash up and help me set the table."

They had barely sat down to eat when Mr. Johnson said, "Maggie, I bought something today that I think you're going to like."

"A pony?" she asked eagerly.

"I'm not telling," he said with a grin. "I want

you to be surprised when the truck comes."

"What truck? When?" Maggie wanted to know.

"Tomorrow," her dad said.

"Morning or afternoon?" she asked.

"John," Mrs. Johnson scolded. "I wish you wouldn't get her so excited about this. We don't want her to be disappointed."

"But *I'm* so excited that I had to say something," he admitted.

"Then tell her the whole story," she urged.

"Not a chance," Maggie's dad said stubbornly. "Everybody likes surprises. Right, Maggie?"

"Oh, yes," Maggie agreed as a grin spread across her face. It had to be a pony! She could hardly wait.

Maggie usually slept until breakfast, but the next morning she was helping her mom in the kitchen long before her dad came in to eat. "I wonder what color he is," she said dreamily.

Her mother looked up from the bacon she was frying. "Who?" she asked.

"The pony," Maggie said.

Her mom frowned and said, "You'll have to ask your father about that."

As soon as Maggie's father had poured milk on

his corn flakes, Maggie asked, "What color is the pony?"

"Did I mention a pony?" he asked innocently.

"Well, no, but . . ." Maggie hesitated.

"Then what pony are you talking about?" her dad asked.

"You said something was coming in a truck today," Maggie said. What else could it be? she wondered.

All morning she kept one eye on the driveway. During lunch she sat next to the window.

Finally Mrs. Johnson said, "Maggie, I want you to help me in the garden this afternoon."

"But, Mom . . ." she protested.

"No buts," her mom cut her off. "You need to think about something besides that truck."

Maggie knew better than to argue. Pulling weeds was bad enough, but she couldn't even see the driveway from the garden. She had just finished weeding the carrots and moved on to the zucchini when she heard a whinny.

Maggie leaped to her feet and raced to the front yard in time to see a big blue truck pull up. It was the type of truck that hauled her dad's cattle to market. A man with a beard was getting out of the truck and Corky was bothering him.

"Corky, be quiet," Maggie yelled as she ran up. "Do you have a pony in there, mister?"

The man chuckled. "Something like that. Is your dad home?" he asked.

"He's in the barn. I'll get him for you," she offered.

But her mom stopped her. "Never mind. Your dad said he would be watching for Mr. Green, and I'm sure he'll be here in a minute," she said.

While Mrs. Johnson talked to the man, Maggie circled the truck. She tried to look in, but the openings between the boards were up too high.

Then her dad came. "Well, hello, Mr. Green," he said, offering his hand. "We can unload right here if you want."

"That will be fine," the man agreed. He reached up just below the truck's back door to pull down a ramp. Maggie's dad helped him carry gates from the sides of the truck to form a chute. Mr. Green started up the chute and opened the back door. Maggie stretched her neck, trying to see what was inside. She caught a flash of gold and big dark eyes.

Then the man was at the top of the ramp with

the biggest horse Maggie had ever seen. It was gold with a white mane and tail. A wide white blaze ran down its face. It was beautiful, but it certainly wasn't a pony.

The ramp shook from the weight of the big animal, and it towered over Maggie's dad. When

Mr. Green appeared with another horse as big as the first, Maggie gasped. "Two horses?" she asked.

Maggie's dad and the man talked excitedly as they led the horses to the barn. Maggie trailed along in a state of shock. She couldn't believe her eyes.

The horses were put in some big stalls that usually held several calves. They snorted at each other and sniffed all around. "What kind of a place is this?" they seemed to say. Soon they found the hay in their mangers and settled down to eat.

"They look happy now," Mr. Green said approvingly. "Good thing you didn't change these stalls when you remodeled your barn."

Maggie's dad nodded. "I guess I've always sort of wanted a team," he said.

Mr. Green smiled. "Draft horses do get in your blood," he said.

"Purebred Belgians would have been nice if they weren't so expensive," Maggie's dad continued.

"I know what you mean. That's why most people do just what you're doing. They buy halfbreds like these first. Your mares will be just as useful, and their foals will still bring good money."

"I hope I can tell them apart," Maggie's dad said cheerfully.

Mr. Green laughed. "When you know them better, you won't have any trouble," he promised. "For now, just remember that Molly is lighter in color than Polly."

"That's good to know," Mr. Johnson nodded.

"Did you talk to Fred Swenson as I suggested?" asked Mr. Green.

"Yes, and I bought all kinds of stuff from him. The goods should be delivered today or tomorrow," Maggie's dad said.

"Good for you. I know you're going to love doing your work with horses. They're more relaxing to use than tractors."

"Sounds good," Maggie's dad said eagerly. "I'll write you a check if you'll come to the house."

When the men were gone, Maggie's mom looked at her daughter. "You've been awfully quiet," she said. "What do you think of our new horses?"

Maggie sniffed. "I wanted a pony of my own,"

she said softly. "These horses belong to Dad."

"I was afraid you might feel that way," her mom said with a sigh. "I begged him not to get your hopes up, but he was sure you'd like them. Sometimes he gets so carried away that I don't know what to do with him."

Maggie didn't answer. She just stared at the horses. They were as big as elephants. What did her dad want with them anyway?

When he returned Mrs. Johnson said, "I'm afraid Maggie is upset about not getting the pony she was expecting."

Her dad's smile died. "But I never said she was getting a pony," he protested. Turning toward Maggie he said, "Besides, a team will be lots better, Maggie. You'll see. They're more useful and dependable. You're going to love their foals."

"They're too big," Maggie shouted. "I can't ride them!"

"But of course you can," her dad insisted. "In the old days all the kids learned to ride on horses like these."

But Maggie wasn't convinced. She *still* wanted a pony.

3

Mr. Johnson brushed the horses before he went to milk the cows that night. He used a brush with teeth in it called a "curry comb" to work up the dirt. He brushed them with a softer brush after that. "Want to try?" he asked, offering Maggie the brush.

She shook her head. They weren't *her* horses.

When her dad left, Maggie went around to the front of the big animals. "At least they're more interesting than cows," she told herself. She reached down and picked up a handful of hay and offered it to Molly. The huge nose sniffed, then Molly took the hay daintily. Long lips popped as the horse reached for more.

Maggie brought more hay and began to feed both horses. They seemed friendly and grateful.

She patted their noses and gave them more to eat. Finally she told them, "That's enough for now. I know Dad fed you, too."

The horses seemed so disappointed that Maggie wanted to get up high enough to pet their heads. Polly saw Maggie begin to climb over the edge of her manger and backed up quickly. The horse's eyes rolled.

Maggie got down. She knew her dad wouldn't like her upsetting his horses. When she tried to climb into Molly's stall things went much better. The light golden mare gave Maggie a friendly sniff and stood very still. Then Maggie played with the horse's thick white mane. The horse closed her eyes when her ears were scratched.

"Well, I'd still rather have a pony," Maggie told Molly at last. "But I guess you'll have to do. I know you can't help being big."

At breakfast the next morning her dad said, "Maggie, would you like to try riding one of our horses today?"

But before Maggie could say anything, her mom cut in. "Oh, John, do you think she should? They're so big. What if she gets stepped on?"

"Betty, Maggie has been around big animals all

her life," he pointed out.

"She never tried to ride a cow," her mom countered.

Mr. Johnson looked smug. "How about that, Maggie? Ever tried to ride a cow?" he asked, his eyes sparkling.

Maggie smiled. "Yes, I did, Mom. Dad put me up on Jeannie once. Cow's backs are really bony."

"I might have known," her mom grinned.

"These horses have nice backs for riding," Maggie's dad assured them. "So how about it?" he asked his daughter.

"Are you sure they're used to being ridden?" Maggie asked suspiciously.

"Of course," said her dad. "I'll get on one of them and prove it if you like."

"Good idea," said Maggie's mom.

"Can we use Molly?" Maggie asked.

Her dad looked surprised. "What difference does it make?" he asked.

"Polly is sort of spooky. She has weird eyes," Maggie told him.

Mr. Johnson shrugged. "Okay. Molly it is. We'll leave Corky in the house so he won't get in our way. Then it's ride 'em, Maggie."

Molly was already wearing a halter, and Maggie's dad slipped the bridle right over it. Polly whinnied frantically as he led her partner out the door, but Molly didn't get upset. Since the Johnsons' didn't have a saddle, Maggie's dad needed something tall to use in order to get on the horse. Holding Molly next to the hay wagon he gave a mighty leap, and he was up.

The horse walked right off when Maggie's dad made a clucking noise with his tongue. He turned her right and left, and they trotted a little. Mr. Johnson and Molly circled back to Maggie.

"This is a good horse," he said as he slid off. "She handles better than most riding horses I've been on. Why, she even neck-reins."

"What's neck-rein?" Maggie wondered.

"That's the way western riders control their horses," he explained. "They use only one hand on the reins so that the other one is free to rope cows." He smiled at Maggie. "Are you ready to ride?"

"I guess so," she answered nervously. "But how am I going to get on?"

"I can push you up," her dad said. He took the

reins and tied them to the wagon. Then Maggie stepped into her father's cupped hands. Before she knew it, she was on top of the huge animal, and it was like sitting on a tall building that breathed. The horse's back was so wide that her legs wouldn't go around it. She was scared.

"Be careful," cautioned Maggie's mom.

"Slide up by her neck," her dad told Maggie. "A horse's body is narrower up there." So Maggie slid forward and grabbed a big handful of mane. Now she felt safer.

"Should I have her walk?" her dad asked.

"Okay, but don't go too fast," Maggie mumbled.

As Molly moved forward, her whole body seemed to twist under Maggie. The girl stiffened, and she held onto the mane for dear life.

"Relax," said her dad. "Let your body go with the horse."

Maggie tried to relax, but it was hard. At last she realized that she hadn't fallen and she probably wouldn't. Riding the big horse didn't seem so scary, and she began to enjoy herself. In fact, she felt lucky and proud. There probably weren't many girls or boys her size who had ridden a horse as big as Molly.

As they started around the yard for the fifth time an old green flatbed truck, hauling a wooden wagon, turned in at their driveway. Mr. Johnson stopped Molly as soon as he saw it. "You'd better get down now," he told Maggie. "That's the new wagon I ordered, and I'll have to help unload it."

Maggie looked down. It was a long way to the ground. Still clutching the mane, she rolled onto her stomach and slid down carefully. Even with her dad's hand guiding her, she landed hard on the ground, and her knees were so wobbly she could barely stand.

"Good morning," boomed a big man with glasses coming toward them. "That sure is a nice horse." His bright blue eyes studied Molly, and his tentlike bib overalls rocked as he moved to consider the horse from every angle.

"Good morning, Swenson," Maggie's dad answered. "I'm glad you brought my wagon so quickly. Now I can start using my new team."

The big man turned to size-up Maggie's dad. "Ever use a team before?" he asked curiously.

"Well, no," Mr. Johnson admitted. "But I did lots of riding as a kid, and Joe Green has given me a lot of help and advice."

"Hmmm," said Mr. Swenson. "A fellow can get hurt around horses if he doesn't know what he's doing."

Maggie's dad frowned and changed the subject. "Did you bring the harnesses?"

"Yes, yes, I did," the big man said, nodding.

"Good. Would you bring them along while I put this horse in her stall?" Mr. Johnson asked.

"Yup. I'll be right with you," said Mr. Swenson. He brought a whole armload of straps and buckles in one hand and two big collars in the other. Putting them carefully on hooks behind the horses, he turned to eye Polly as thoroughly as he had Molly. "This one is even better," he decided. "If you ever decide to sell these horses, I'd like first chance."

"I'll keep you in mind," Mr. Johnson promised. "Now we'd better get that wagon unloaded."

* * * * * *

Mr. Swenson and his truck were barely out of sight when Mr. Johnson said, "Maggie, get your mother. We're going for a wagon ride."

"This I've got to see," her mom said as soon as Maggie told her what her dad had said. In the barn they found Molly wearing a completely tangled mess of leather. Mr. Johnson was looking confused.

"That doesn't look quite right," Maggie's mom observed.

Mr. Johnson looked at them sheepishly. "It isn't," he admitted, "and I can't figure it out."

Maggie's mom shook her head. "And you said you knew all about horses. I wish you'd never bought this team."

"Mr. Swenson said he'd like to buy them," Maggie offered. "And a pony would be lots cheaper."

"Never mind, Maggie," snapped her dad.

4

"Well, what are you going to do about getting those horses harnessed?" Mrs. Johnson insisted at breakfast the next morning.

"I'll run over to Clara City tomorrow and get a few more pointers from Mr. Green," Maggie's dad announced.

"Only if Maggie and I get to go along," her mom said firmly. "I've heard so much about that man's horses that I want to see them for myself."

"I've got to get to work now," Mr. Johnson said. He helped clear the breakfast dishes. Then he went out the back door and headed toward the barn. Maggie was right behind him. "First we'll put these horses in the pasture. Maggie, would you please open the door? Watch out and don't get in the way."

Maggie swung the heavy barn door open and stood back to watch. The horses started toward the door with their nostrils flaring. Once outside, they began to run in circles with short bouncy steps. Suddenly Polly's head went up. Her eyes were rivoted on the cows gathered by the water tank. She seemed to talk things over with Molly, and then, both went off toward the cows at a cautious trot. As the horses picked up speed, the cows looked up to see the strange, new animals bearing down on them at a gallop. Water flew as the herd scattered.

"Hey, stop that," Mr. Johnson yelled. He charged out of the barn to defend his cows with Maggie right behind. "Look out," he cried, grabbing his daughter just in time to save her from being trampled by a wild-eyed heifer. "Get out of here," he bellowed. He waved his arms at a playful horse that was hot on the cow's tail.

Maggie knew at once that she shouldn't have followed her dad this time. Even he wasn't safe in this stampede. "Stay close to me," he told her, and he waved his arms frantically at the animals while moving back to the barn. Then he pushed Maggie inside the door to safety and grabbed a pitchfork before returning to the battle.

The horses knew the fun was over as soon as they saw the pitchfork. They headed down the lane toward the pasture at a trot. The cows settled down, and Maggie's dad went to get his tractor. "I hope none of these critters goes through a fence," he said glumly. "I'll just have to keep an eye on them while I do my work, I guess."

That afternoon Maggie's mom announced she was going shopping. Maggie asked immediately, "Can you drop me at Kelly Davis's?" Knowing how much Maggie missed seeing her friend from school, her mom quickly agreed.

Both girls were crazy about horses, and they usually spent their time together playing with Kelly's huge collection of models. Today she had something really special to show Maggie.

"Dad had it made just for me," Kelly explained as she brought out a small wooden stable. There were eight box stalls, places to hang bridles and saddles, and tiny mangers filled with Easter-basket hay.

Maggie loved it. "Wow. That's fantastic," she told Kelly, and she dropped to her knees to

admire the way the doors opened on their tiny hinges. "We've got something new at our house, too."

"Is it an animal?" Kelly asked eagerly. "You're so lucky to live on a farm."

"Uh huh. Dad bought two great big horses," she said.

"He did?" Kelly exploded. "Two horses? Well, tell me all about them. What are their names? What do they look like?" she asked.

Maggie was pleased with her friend's reaction. "Their names are Polly and Molly, and they're golden brown with white manes and tails."

"Oh, how exciting! Maybe we can each ride one and go all over the countryside this summer," Kelly suggested.

"Well, I don't know about that," Maggie said doubtfully. "Dad really bought them to work in the fields."

"Then they're not riding horses," Kelly realized.

Maggie shook her head. "No, but Dad let me sit on Molly yesterday. He seems to think I'll be able to ride her."

"When can I see them?" Kelly asked.

"Whenever you want," Maggie told her.

"Tomorrow?"

"Gee, we won't be home tomorrow," Maggie remembered. "We're going to Clara City to the farm where our horses came from. Why don't you come along?"

"Oh, I'd love to," Kelly said excitedly. "Do you

think your parents would mind?"

"No, they won't care. Let's ask your mom about it right now," Maggie said.

Both mothers said "yes," and Maggie was in a good mood as she went after the cows that evening. Her efforts to bring the cows home were doomed to failure. When she walked to circle behind the herd, the horses eyed her suspiciously and trotted off. Maggie got all the cows headed in the right direction only to have the horses come charging back to scatter them. She tried again and again, but the job was impossible. Finally she went storming to the house to tell her dad.

"Okay, okay," he told her sourly. "I'll come out and help you." He got a bucket of oats and set off with such long strides that Maggie had to run to keep up.

The horses saw the bucket and followed Mr. Johnson. The cows followed the horses, and Maggie followed the cows. By the time the whole procession reached home, Mr. Johnson was very late with the milking. As he quickly threw feed to the cattle, Maggie asked softly, "Don't you wish I'd had a pony tonight?" But her dad pretended not to hear.

* * * * * *

The next day the girls and Mrs. Johnson had plenty of time to admire Mr. Green's horses while Maggie's dad talked to the man. "Even the foals are huge," her mom observed.

"You mean some of those are foals?" Kelly asked doubtfully.

"Sure," Maggie told her. "They may be as big as most riding horses, but only the babies have those long legs and short tails."

"I love to watch them play," said Maggie's mom, chuckling at the game of tag in progress.

After a while Mr. Green shook his head and said, "John, I think you ought to show me what you're talking about. You ladies can come, too."

They followed Mr. Green inside the barn. There was a long row of stalls. A brass nameplate and a shiny harness hung behind each one. In the first stall stood the biggest horse they had seen, yet.

"Try putting a harness on old Barney here," Mr. Green suggested.

So Maggie's dad got a collar and buckled it onto the huge horse's neck. He lifted down the harness and struggled to get the mass of straps and buckles over the broad back. Centering the harness, he fastened a buckle before he stopped and shook his head.

Maggie had been watching Mr. Green as her dad worked, and she had seen the man start to smile. The more her dad struggled, the more Mr. Green grinned. Finally he began to laugh out loud.

Mr. Johnson looked around and shifted his weight uncomfortably. He reminded Maggie of the boys at school when they didn't know the answer to an arithmetic problem. Mrs. Johnson and Kelly seemed puzzled about the laughter, too.

Finally Mr. Green stopped laughing and wiped his eyes. "I'm sorry," he apologized. "It's just that I never saw anyone put a harness on like that before. John, you've got it inside out!"

"Inside out?" the Johnsons echoed.

"Yup," said Mr. Green, going to help Maggie's dad. "The side of the harness that hangs against the wall is the side you put against the horse. As you threw the harness on, you turned it over. I'd call that inside out, wouldn't you?" Now Maggie's dad looked really embarrassed.

* * * * * *

It was past milking time when the Johnsons drove into their driveway. "I'd better help you with the cows tonight," Mr. Johnson said to Maggie with a sigh. "No telling what kind of a mess we'll have with those horses."

This time Maggie's dad brought a bridle, as well as oats, when he set off for the pasture. He captured Molly and stepped on a large rock so that he could swing up on the horse's back.

"Can I ride, too?" Maggie asked.

"No, that would be too dangerous," he said, reining Molly toward the nearest cow. The cow moved quickly for Mr. Johnson and his cow horse.

"Nuts," muttered Maggie. "I'm the one who wanted a pony."

Soon all the cows started toward the barn at a very fast walk. Polly trotted along behind Molly, and Maggie was left behind. Then she saw all the animals trot, and then they began to gallop. Molly's rear end seemed to be bouncing high off the ground and Mr. Johnson was bouncing even higher. All at once he seemed to be slipping to one side.

"Oh, no," Maggie shouted. "Watch out, Dad!"

5

Maggie saw her father hit the ground. She ran to him as fast as her legs could go. She prayed he wasn't hurt and sure enough, before she could reach him, he was on his feet. He was dusting himself off and feeling one shoulder as she asked breathlessly, "Dad, are you all right?"

Wincing, he said, "I think so, but I'm going to be a little stiff for the next few days."

"What happened?" Maggie asked.

"I think maybe I'm too old to play cowboy. You won't tell your mother about this, will you?" he asked, grinning.

Maggie laughed and promised she wouldn't.

After seeing her dad fall off, Maggie was a little nervous about riding Molly again. He assured her that Molly would never have acted that way if the cows hadn't started running. She soon realized he was right and eagerly went back to riding the horse any time her dad would lead Molly around the yard. Every time she rode, Maggie gained confidence, but her chances to ride were few. Her dad was just too busy with his fieldwork now.

One Sunday, Maggie convinced her father to let her ride Molly by herself.

When they got to the barn Mr. Johnson put his daughter up on Molly and announced, "Today you're going to learn to control that moose. If you neck-rein her, you'll even have an extra hand to use on her mane."

Maggie put both reins in one hand. Her dad put his own hand over hers to demonstrate what to do. "If you want to go to the right, reach your hand up along Molly's neck like this," he said.

With her dad's strong arm helping, Molly moved obediently to the right. "Got it?" he asked, letting go of her hand. Maggie nodded her head. "Good. Now we'll walk forward so you can try it," he added.

As Molly walked, Maggie tried to make the horse move to the right. But no matter how hard she shoved or pulled, Molly ignored her. The big horse just kept following her dad. Maggie tried again and again to make Molly move to the right. But still the horse wouldn't turn.

Mr. Johnson came back and put his hand over Maggie's again. "Reach farther forward on the reins like this," he directed. "Molly's neck is so thick that she probably can't feel the directions you're giving her from back there." Then he walked forward again with Molly following.

Maggie pulled left on the reins harder than ever. But the mare just kept plodding ahead as if she hadn't noticed her rider. "Want to give up?" her dad asked at last.

Maggie shook her head, "no." There has to be a way to get Molly's attention, she thought. She took the right rein in her hand and pulled with all her might. At the same time she kicked the stubborn horse with her right foot. Amazingly, Molly turned.

"Yippee," cried Maggie. "I did it!"

"You sure did," cheered her dad. "That wasn't neck-reining, that was determination. Good girl."

Maggie was pretty proud of herself. They tried more turns in both directions. Then her dad showed her how to start and stop the horse.

Stopping was easy. Molly came to a halt as soon as Maggie said, "Whoa." But then the horse seemed to fall asleep, and Maggie couldn't get her started again.

"Get up," said Maggie, adding a clucking sound. Nothing happened. "Get up," she said more firmly and nudged Molly with her heels. Still nothing happened.

Now Maggie was getting angry. Why won't Molly listen when I ask nicely? she wondered. "Get up!" she bellowed, and booted the horse as hard as she could. Molly's head came up, and she lurched into motion.

Mr. Johnson began to laugh. "I never knew my daughter was such a tough customer," he said cheerfully. "There's no way someone your size can hurt that big horse, so I'm on your side. Do whatever you can to get Molly to move. Just don't let her stop until you're ready."

But before her dad had finished speaking, Molly had coasted to a stop. Maggie pounded the mare with both feet and yelled at her, "Get up, you lazy beast!" Molly moved out and did not stop again until Maggie decided that she should.

"Good girl," said Maggie, giving the horse a

pat. "It's fun riding you, but I seem to be doing most of the work."

"You're right," her dad agreed. "Any horse will seem easy to ride after this one."

As Maggie slid off Molly, a big blue car pulled into the driveway. "I wonder who that can be," said Mr. Johnson.

"Oh, it's Kelly," cried Maggie, racing toward her friend. "Did you see me riding? Isn't Molly pretty?" asked Maggie as Kelly stepped out of the car.

"Yes, I saw you, and she is beautiful," said Kelly, not going any closer to the horse. "But she's so big." Kelly's eyes grew wide.

"Want to ride?" Maggie asked eagerly.

"Oh, no, thank you anyway," said Mrs. Davis, hurrying up. "We just stopped to see the horses."

"But it's fun, Kelly," Maggie urged. "Molly is really gentle."

"And very safe," her dad added. "I'd be glad to lead the horse around for you."

"No, really. I don't want to," Kelly said quickly. "Thanks anyway."

Maggie frowned. "Are you sure? You'd like it, I know you would." She had really been counting on sharing Molly with her best friend. But Kelly's mind was made up. She finally agreed to pet Molly, but that was all. The horse was just too big.

* * * * * *

The next morning Maggie's dad took the team out to cultivate corn. When he came in for lunch, Mrs. Johnson asked, "How did the horses do?"

"They're stepping on a lot of corn," he confessed. "But I ought to be steering them right, soon."

A few days later all the hay wagons were full, and Maggie's dad still had a few bales left in the field. "I think I'll use the team to get the rest," he told his wife. "You can come, too, Maggie, and help me drive the wagon."

She didn't need to be asked twice. "Sure!" she cried, leaping from the table to follow.

As soon as they reached the first group of hay bales, Mr. Johnson handed the reins to Maggie. He loaded the hay and said, "Okay, Maggie, follow me."

"Get up," said Maggie, slapping the reins

against the horses' backs. They stepped right off and brought the wagon to the next group of bales. Maggie's dad threw the hay on the back, and the horses moved on. The job went smoothly.

When the wagon was full, her dad said, "Time to go home, eh, Mike?"

Maggie looked puzzled. "Mike?" she asked.

Her dad laughed. "Sure. You're my hired hand, aren't you? Whoever heard of a hired hand named Maggie?" he asked.

The trip home seemed to take a long time. "Mr. Green said I'd find these horses relaxing, but I think they're just plain slow," Mr. Johnson complained.

"It's a hot day. Maybe they're tired," said Maggie.

But her dad didn't answer. His attention was on the cornfield they were passing. He stopped the team and stood up to see better. Maggie stood up and looked, too. Suddenly she noticed a flash of black and white moving among the green stalks. The cows were in the corn!

About the same time, Polly also noticed the movement. The frightened horse bolted forward so strongly that both Maggie and her father were thrown backward onto the wagon. The reins yanked out of her dad's hands. The wagon had become a runaway, and her dad was powerless to stop it!

Bales flew in all directions as the wagon careened toward the barn. The wagon nearly overturned as the team came to a sudden stop after swerving to the right. Luckily the barn door

was closed, or the horses would have wrecked the wagon and part of the barn trying to get in. Her dad leaped out of the wagon and ran to the heads of his snorting team.

"Darn crazy animals," he fumed. "I've got to get the cows out of the corn before they ruin everything, but I can't leave these two just standing here. Run and get your mother, Maggie. Tell her to bring Corky, too. We're going to need all the help we can get."

So Maggie ran to the house while her dad put the horses away. Then the whole family jumped into the pickup for a wild ride to the cornfield. Mr. Johnson handed them each a club and said, "There's nothing harder to handle than cows that have tasted corn, so stick together. We'll start at this end of the field, a few rows apart, and try to get them headed toward the barnyard.

The Johnsons started down the corn rows yelling and making as much noise as possible. For once Corky's barking was welcome.

"Get out of here!" Maggie's dad yelled as they approached the first two cows. When the animals just sort of danced around and kept stepping on corn, he swung his club furiously.

The cows galloped off with their tails high in the air. They wanted to cut back behind the Johnsons, but Maggie's mom ran to head them off on her end. When the cows came toward Maggie, she clobbered one right on the nose. It was hard to believe that these were the same lazy animals that she brought home every night.

Maggie and her parents ran until they thought their lungs would burst. Sometimes they fell on uneven ground. Once a cow knocked her mother down. Still the battle raged. Finally every cow was again safely in the barnyard.

The Johnsons fell exhausted in a heap of hay bales. No one had the strength to say anything for a long time. "Whew," her mom said at last. "Life is never dull around here."

"It sure isn't," said Mr. Johnson. "And I'm sure this bit of excitement cost a bunch of money in ruined corn." Maggie's dad was very quiet. She knew he was miserable. There would be no chance for a good yield in that field.

6

The better Maggie got at riding the more she wished she could get on Molly by herself. Her dad never had time for her any more. The horses were always out in the field now because they worked too slow for her dad. Maggie suddenly decided to go to the pasture and work on her riding.

She found Polly and Molly stretched out under an oak tree. They were even snoring. Maggie had thought horses slept standing up. Now she knew they sometimes didn't.

"Hello. Having a good nap?" she asked loudly.

The horses jerked their bodies into an upright position and looked around. When they realized the voice was Maggie's, they stretched and yawned.

Maggie walked right up to Molly and put her arm around the mare's neck. She waited to see if the animal would get up after all, but Molly only yawned again.

"This is my perfect chance," Maggie told herself excitedly. Carefully she leaned on the horse's back. It would be easy to get on, but it might be dangerous, she realized. She had no bridle to control Molly. What would the horse do? Maggie wondered. She hesitated a long time before deciding.

Maggie put one leg over the horse's broad back and pulled herself on. Desperately she maneuvered her body up next to Molly's neck. Nervously she waited to see what the horse would do.

But Molly seemed not to have noticed her at all. Gradually Maggie relaxed. She realized that when Molly was lying down, she was almost the size of the pony Maggie had asked for in the first place.

Maggie pretended to herd cows as she sat on Molly's back. When Maggie got tired of that, she imagined riding Molly in the Kentucky Derby. Later, Molly's broad back made a soft couch to lay on while Maggie studied the clouds.

Suddenly Maggie heard barking right next to her. The horse's front end shot up as she rose quickly to her feet.

Maggie made one frantic grab for Molly's mane, but she missed. Instead, she slid down along the horse's back and landed on the ground. She didn't get hurt, but it was sort of a shock to be gazing up at two huge legs.

Corky was still barking at the horse, and Molly turned to stand guard over Maggie. The big horse stamped her feet and charged the noisy dog while keeping a worried eye on her fallen rider.

Maggie got up quickly and gave Molly a pat. "It's all right, girl," she told the horse. "That silly dog won't hurt me or you, but you were good to take care of me."

Molly relaxed and went to graze. Discouraged, Maggie dusted off her seat. "Next time I'll make sure I'm not followed," she announced as she grabbed Corky and headed home.

* * * * * *

Maggie was watching T.V. that evening when

the phone rang. It was Aunt Jane to say that she and the kids would be out the next day.

"Wait until Tim and Jamie see the horses!" Maggie told her parents. "They're going to be surprised." But then she had another thought. Gee, I bragged about a pony. What will they say about a team of horses?

Tim and Jamie were out of the car before Aunt Jane had turned off the engine. "Hey, Maggie," Jamie said excitedly. "Dad bought us model airplanes that really fly."

"We'll show you how to fly them," Tim added.

"Would you like to see our new horses first?" Maggie asked quietly.

Tim's eyes opened wide. "Horses? Horses? Where?" he demanded.

"I want to see them, too," Jamie agreed.

"They're in the barn," Maggie said. She started toward the barn, but Tim and Jamie passed her immediately. She had to run to keep up.

Mr. Johnson met them at the door and barred their way. "Hey, hey, slow down," he cautioned them. "You can't go running around horses like that. You'll get them upset."

Tim and Jamie looked sorry and tiptoed into

the barn. Jamie whispered, pointing, "They're over there. Look how big they are!"

"They're . . . enormous," gasped Tim. "I thought Maggie was getting a pony."

"Oh, these horses are much better than a pony," Maggie's dad told them. "Not only can you ride them, but they can work in the field and pull wagons."

"Do you have saddles for them?" Jamie asked.

Her uncle laughed. "I don't think they make saddles that big," he said. "You don't need to use a saddle anyway."

"Are they fast?" asked Tim.

"Fast enough for you guys," Maggie's dad answered. "Maggie, why don't you get a bridle, and we'll show them how these big horses move."

When his uncle began to put the bridle in place, Tim got all excited. "Golly," he exclaimed. "You put your hand right into that horse's mouth. Doesn't she bite?" he asked.

"Of course not," Maggie told him. "Molly is a good horse."

"Besides, she doesn't have any teeth where I put my hand," her dad added. "Come here, and I'll show you."

Tim backed away. "No, that's all right," he said. "I'll take your word for it."

"Let me see," said Jamie, scrambling to her uncle's side. A look of wonder crossed her face as her uncle showed her just where to put her hand. "Gosh, that's neat. I wonder if that's how lion tamers do it," she said.

Maggie's dad shook his head and grinned. "No, Jamie. Lions have a lot more teeth than Molly does, so don't get any ideas." He buckled the straps on the bridle and said, "All right, everyone outside." As Tim started to run, Mr. Johnson added, "And please walk."

Aunt Jane was ready with her camera. Tim and Jamie were ready to ride. Maggie was feeling a little left out.

"Why don't you let Maggie ride first," suggested Aunt Jane. "She can show us how it's done."

That made Maggie feel a lot better. At last she had something special that her cousins knew nothing about. She rode around the yard and then her dad made her get down.

"Now it's my turn," Tim insisted. "Can we gallop?"

"Let's try a walk first," his uncle said, as he boosted the boy up. "Slide forward and get ahold of the mane."

Tim grabbed Molly's mane in both hands, and

began to wiggle his body. "Giddy up," he said eagerly.

Maggie's dad walked forward with Molly, and immediately Tim's face changed. "Steady, horse. Not so fast," he said nervously. His smile returned before long, however. Then he was bubbling, "Mom, this is great. Can we have a horse?"

Maggie's Aunt Jane groaned. "That's all we need. We've got a dog, a cat and two gerbils. Where would we put a horse? In the laundry room?" she asked.

"Horses are very expensive pets," Maggie's mom added.

"Jamie's turn now," Maggie's dad announced.

"Can I ride again after she's done?" Tim pleaded. "I want to ride by myself like Maggie did."

"We'll see," Maggie's dad answered, pulling Tim off.

As soon as Jamie was on she hugged Molly around the neck and gave her a kiss. She too was a little nervous at first, but soon her face seemed to glow with happiness. "I want to do this forever," Jamie sighed.

"Sorry," said her uncle. "Your old uncle can't quite manage that. I think you'd better get down now."

"It's my turn again," Tim reminded him. "You promised I could ride by myself this time."

"Funny," said Maggie's dad, shaking his head. "I don't remember making that promise. Tell you what, why don't we have Molly give everyone a wagon ride instead?" he asked.

"That's a wonderful idea," said Tim's mom before he could complain. "That's much better than riding bareback."

Tim made a face and whispered to Maggie, "Boy, are you lucky. I wish I could ride the way you do."

Even Aunt Jane took a turn at driving the team and wagon. Maggie's dad offered his daughter a chance, too. But now driving didn't seem so special to her.

When Maggie's dad finally said that he had to get back to his fieldwork, the women headed off toward the house. The kids went to fly the model planes behind the barn.

As they walked along, Jamie kept looking at Maggie. "How often do you get to ride the horse?" she asked at last.

"Almost every day," Maggie exaggerated.

"Oh, I wish I were you," the younger girl exclaimed.

"Well, it's still not like having a pony of your own," Tim pointed out. "You'll never be able to get on those big horses alone."

Maggie felt like telling him about her adventure in the pasture, but she knew Tim. If he heard about her getting on Molly's back, he'd want to try it, too. Maggie wasn't ready to share Molly with anyone, any more than she had to.

7

The day after her cousins' visit, Maggie headed down the lane for another secret pasture ride. This time the horses were standing head-to-tail under the oak tree. Polly was keeping the flies off Molly's nose, and Molly returned the favor. Today's ride was going to take more planning.

Maggie looked around the pasture for ideas on how to get on Molly. The rock her dad had used wasn't too far away, but it was too low for someone her size. The barbed wire fence around the field was tall enough, but she certainly couldn't stand on that. If only they had wooden fences.

"Wooden fences?" she asked herself. There used to be an old wooden gate at the far end of the pasture. That might work.

The saggy old gate was nearly hidden by tall grass and a low hanging maple tree. Maggie wondered if its wood was too rotten to support her weight. She scurried up the cross pieces to find out.

The gate turned out to be sturdier than she had expected. Better yet, one of the maple's limbs hung in just the right place for Maggie to steady herself at the top. If she could get Molly to stand close enough to the gate, her plan would work.

The horses were still dozing in the shade, so Maggie had no trouble grabbing Molly's halter. The horse, however, planted her feet and refused to go anywhere. What Maggie needed was a bribe.

Next time, she thought, I'll bring some oats. What else would tempt a stubborn horse? she wondered. She saw clover blooming in the field beyond the fence. She slipped through the three sharp strands of wire to pick the clover and to find out if her plan would work on Molly.

Molly was definitely interested in the clover, but so was Polly. When the horses started kicking at each other, Maggie drew back and waited until it was clear that Polly would not share the treat.

Getting Molly to the gate was much easier than making her stand in just the right position. She would bring her head next to the gate, but not her back. It was a real balancing act for Maggie as she tried to hold the clover in just the right spot.

Then, for a split second, the horse's back was close enough to the gate, and Maggie began to slide on. As she did, Molly moved. It was just enough to leave Maggie hanging by one hand and one knee. Maggie had barely gotten over that scare when Molly curled her head around looking for more clover. That caused the horse's back to tilt drastically, and Maggie managed to climb on. Then, Molly made a grunting sound and began walking.

"I did it!" Maggie told the world. "I'm riding all by myself, and I don't care where we go!"

Her ride was very short, however, because Molly soon dropped her head to graze. There was nothing Maggie could do about it. She couldn't even pretend to be an Indian scout or a circus bareback rider on a horse that's grazing. When it was obvious that Molly might go on eating for a long time, Maggie gave up. She decided to find a way to control Molly before she tried pasture riding again.

The next day her dad agreed to help Maggie with her riding. She insisted that he teach her

how to put on Molly's bridle.

"But you can't reach high enough to put the bridle over her head," he pointed out.

"Then she'll just have to keep her head down," said Maggie.

"What if she won't?" her dad asked.

"I'll feed her some oats while I'm doing it," she insisted.

Her dad shrugged his shoulders. He could see that his daughter's mind was made up. "Okay," he said, showing her how to hold the top of the bridle in her right hand. "Be sure to keep it up high, like this, so that everything hangs straight. Then offer her the bit and the oats with your left hand, and you should be able to slip in the bit. The hardest part will be to get the top of the bridle over her ears before she spits the bit out again."

Sure enough, Molly managed to spit out the bit on Maggie's first two tries. The third try was more successful, only because her dad held the horse's head down.

Panting and proud, Maggie said, "If I were about three feet taller, it would be easy."

"Yup," her dad agreed. "That's just what I

need, a daughter seven feet tall. Are you ready to ride yet?" he asked.

Maggie nodded and let him throw her on the horse. She was already plotting her next pasture ride. With a bridle she'd have control of Molly, but she was going to need help to put the bridle on.

Her mom came along just as her dad was turning the horses loose for the day. "Well, I see the beasts are at least giving pony rides again," she observed. "That's about the only thing they do that's useful."

"I'll probably be using them tomorrow," Maggie's dad said quickly. "They can help haul straw bales."

Her mom made a big sigh and walked off. Maggie thought, I like the horses! They're neat! Mom will soon like them, too. Even Dad's learned to have patience with them.

Maggie hoped her dad would continue to ignore her mother's complaints.

That afternoon Maggie and her mom drove into town. As they stopped at the grocery store for a few items, she asked, "Mom, can we stop at Kelly's after this?"

"Oh, Maggie, we can't stop every time," her mom objected.

"But I've got to ask her something," Maggie insisted.

Her mother looked at her watch and sighed. "All right," she agreed, "But we'll only stay a few minutes. I need to get home and start supper."

As soon as the Johnsons arrived, the girls headed for Kelly's room. "I can ride Molly in the pasture all by myself now," Maggie told her excitedly. "If you'll come out and help me bridle her, we can ride all afternoon."

Kelly was not enthusiastic. "She's too big. We'd get hurt," she said.

"No, we wouldn't. Come on," Maggie urged.

"If you had a pony, I'd be at your house all the time," Kelly answered. "But you're going to get hurt if you keep messing around with that workhorse."

"No, I won't," Maggie protested. "Molly is very gentle. Honest."

"Time to go," called Mrs. Johnson.

"Just a minute," Maggie called back. "Please, Kelly, say you'll come this week. I really need your help."

Kelly shook her head, "No."

"Maggie," called her mom.

"All right," Maggie answered. Turning back to Kelly, she said, "If you're going to be a chicken, I'll just have to find someone else to ride with me."

* * * * * *

The Johnson family went to the Andersons' for dinner that Sunday. Tim and Jamie had many new things to show Maggie as usual, but they also wanted to hear more about the horses.

"Dad never leads Molly when I ride her now," she told them. "He even showed me how to bridle her myself."

"Boy, are you lucky," said Jamie.

Maggie nodded. "And guess what else," she said very softly.

"What?" her cousins wanted to know.

"Can you keep a secret?" she asked, looking around to see who was listening.

They nodded eagerly.

"I've been on Molly twice all by myself, and my folks don't even know about it," she whispered.

"How did you manage that?" Tim asked suspiciously.

"The first time I caught Molly lying down so I just crawled on," she said.

"Then what happened?" Jamie insisted.

"Corky came along barking, and she got up really fast. I slid right off her rump," Maggie grinned.

Tim and Jamie giggled over that for a long time. Then Tim said, "Tell us about the second time."

Maggie was enjoying telling her story. "The next time I got Molly to stand next to an old gate, and I just jumped on."

"Neat!" Jamie exclaimed.

"Shhh," warned Maggie. "It was pretty neat, except that she didn't have a bridle, so I had no way of making her go where I wanted her to go."

"That's not so neat," Tim said quickly. "Where did she take you?"

Maggie said grimly, "Nowhere. She just stood around eating. I got tired of it and finally got off her."

"What a bummer," said Tim. "You didn't get off to a very good start."

"I'll say," she agreed. "Now you see why I had Dad teach me to put the bridle on. Next time will be different."

"That was good thinking," said Tim. "So when are you going to try to ride again?"

"I want to try it really soon, but I still have a problem," she admitted. "I can't get the bridle on unless she keeps her head down, and I can't be sure she'll cooperate."

Tim looked interested. "Maybe Jamie and I could help you. If we help you keep the horse's head down, would you let us ride by ourselves, too?"

Maggie had to think about that. She really hated to share Molly with Tim because he was so reckless, but at least he wasn't afraid.

At last she asked, "When could you come out?"

"Maybe Wednesday," Tim said. "I don't think Mom has anything planned for that day."

"Okay," Maggie schemed. "If you can get your mom to bring you out, we'll tackle Molly together."

8

After breakfast on Monday, Mr. Johnson mentioned he would be fixing fence. "I really should bale the rest of the straw before it rains instead," he grumbled. "But those darn cows will be in the corn again if I don't fix that fence today."

"I noticed you used the tractor for that straw you baled on Saturday," Maggie's mom said pointedly.

Maggie's dad turned angrily. "And I'll be using the horses for the fencing," he snapped, jamming on his hat and heading for the door. Just before the door slammed, he called back, "Maggie, I'll need your help."

Luckily the horses were close by. It didn't take long to catch them, but Maggie's dad was still in a bad mood. He slapped the harnesses on in a careless way. When Polly moved around, he bellowed, "Stand still or I'll smack you."

Out by the wagon, Maggie held the horses while he walked around to hook up. "Doggone it. I'm missing a trace chain," he fumed loudly. Polly raised her head nervously.

"I'll have to see if I can find another one," he continued, as he disappeared into the barn.

Maggie was left holding the horses. She waited and waited, and she wondered what was taking her dad so long. When the horses began to fall asleep, she began to yawn, too.

Suddenly her dad burst through a seldom-used door just behind the team. A bunch of fence posts swung crazily in his arms. Even Maggie jumped a little.

Suddenly Polly panicked and leaped forward knocking Maggie to the ground.

"Owwww," she wailed as her ankle bent under her. The pain was intense. She cried out again, grabbing her ankle.

Her dad dropped the fence posts and hurried to her. "Oh, my gosh," he groaned. "I never thought about scaring those crazy horses. Are you all right, Maggie?" he asked.

But Maggie was crying too hard to answer. She rocked back and forth on the ground holding her injured ankle.

"Let's get the shoe off," he ordered.

"Oh, no. Don't! It hurts," she screamed as he fiddled with her shoe laces.

"It's swelling badly already," he muttered. "I'd better get you to the house." With that he scooped up Maggie and walked quickly toward the house. "Betty, Betty, come here!" he yelled as he went.

Mrs. Johnson raced out the door. "What's the matter? What happened? For goodness sake, tell me what happened," she urged.

"It's Maggie," Mr. Johnson panted. "The horses ran her down, and she's complaining about her ankle. Now the team is running all over the yard and I've got to catch them before they hurt themselves." Then he laid Maggie on the porch and hurried off.

"Oh, no," gasped her mom, bending to have a look. "Those darn horses. All they are is trouble. We'd better get ice on this right away."

Maggie didn't want ice, but her mom insisted. "I know it hurts, Honey, but it will keep the swelling down," she said gently.

Her dad came back in time to drive them to the doctor's office. Maggie's ankle hurt so much that the trip seemed to take forever. When Dr. Holland insisted on X rays, they had to go to the emergency room at the hospital.

At last the blonde technician had taken pictures of Maggie's throbbing ankle and a doctor with a moustache brought them the results.

"Your foot is not broken after all," he said cheerfully. "But it is going to be painful for a while, so I will give you some pills to take home." He turned to Maggie's parents and said, "Our young lady is to soak her ankle in very hot water three times a day and to stay off of it. Any questions?"

They shook their heads, and soon they were on their way home again. Maggie cried quietly in the back seat, because her ankle hurt badly. She could vaguely hear her parents talking.

"I'm beginning to agree with you, Betty," said Mr. Johnson. "I think I'll see if that Mr. Swenson is still interested in buying the horses."

"No, you can't sell Molly," Maggie protested weakly. "I love her," she sobbed.

"Those horses are dangerous and expensive," her mom said firmly. "The sooner we get rid of them, the better I'll like it."

"But, Mom . . ." Maggie wailed. Tears spilled down her cheeks.

"I'll call Swenson when I'm in Brownstown next week," said Maggie's dad.

* * * * * *

Maggie had forgotten all about her deal with Tim and Jamie until they appeared two days later. "Gosh, your foot is all blue and wrinkly," Tim observed. "It looks gross."

"I know," Maggie said glumly. "You should have seen it Monday. It was practically purple."

"Does it hurt?" asked Jamie.

"No, not too bad. I just feel stiff and sore," she said.

"What about Molly?" Tim asked softly.

Maggie made a face. "What do you think? I can't even walk, and now Dad is talking about selling the team."

"How come?" Jamie protested. "Molly is a really neat horse."

"Oh, Mom's been complaining about how little they do, and I guess my getting hurt didn't help."

"Do you think he'll do anything right away?"

Tim wanted to know.

"Dad's going to talk to someone about buying the horses next week," she explained.

"Just when we had such a neat plan," he complained. "How long before you can walk again?"

"A few days, I guess. Do you think your mom would bring you out again soon?" Maggie asked.

Tim looked doubtful. "She's going to wonder what we're up to if we push her too hard," he said.

Maggie thought and thought. Then she had an idea. "Mom was saying just the other day that the blackberries will be ripe soon," she said eagerly. "Would your mom come out to pick those?"

Tim's face brightened. "She might if your mom invited her."

"Let's ask her right away," Jamie said excitedly.

"No," Tim cautioned. "We've got to play this cool. We'll wait until supper, and I'll do the talking."

* * * * * *

All during supper Maggie waited for Tim to say something about blackberries, but he seemed to have forgotten about their idea. Then, as everyone was enjoying his aunt's apple pie, he said casually, "This is really good, Aunt Betty. But do you know what my most favorite pie is?"

"What's that?" she asked.

"Blackberry," Tim gushed. "I just love blackberry pie."

Aunt Jane looked surprised. "I never knew that. You never mentioned it before," she said.

Then, right on cue, Maggie's mom said, "Oh, Jane, speaking of blackberries . . . There are going to be a lot of them this year. Why don't you come out and go picking with me? Bring the children along, of course."

Aunt Jane smiled eagerly. "That sounds like fun. I haven't picked blackberries in years. When will they be ready?"

"In about a week."

"We'll be here," said Aunt Jane.

Tim gave Maggie a sly wink from behind the milk pitcher.

9

Mr. Johnson was returning from a trip to Brownstown a few days later when Maggie hobbled out to meet him. Smiling, he told her, "Swenson is still interested in our horses, and he'll be over tomorrow for another look. We didn't talk price, but it looks good."

Maggie's heart sank. "Dad, please don't sell Molly now," she pleaded. "I want to keep her."

"Honey, buying that team was a mistake from the beginning," he said firmly. "We can't afford to keep them as pets."

"Then sell Polly and keep Molly," she suggested.

"It doesn't work that way," he replied. "They're a team, and they stay together."

"But, Dad, this isn't fair," wailed Maggie,

pulling on his sleeve to make him listen.

"I'm sorry," he said evenly. "Life isn't always fair. We tried the team and they're just not working out."

"But, Dad . . ." she pleaded. Maggie began to cry as her father strode toward the house without looking back.

The next morning the horses did not go out to pasture. Instead, Maggie's dad brushed until their coats were so shiny that Maggie knew Swenson would buy them. Maybe they'll be too expensive for him, she thought hopefully. But she knew that her dad planned to ask only what he'd paid for them. Swenson would probably agree.

Maybe if he saw how spooky Polly could be . . . Maybe if something or someone happened to scare her at just the right time . . .

As if Mr. Johnson knew what his daughter was thinking, he said, "Maggie, when Mr. Swenson comes, I want you to go into the house."

"Why?" she wanted to know.

"You might do or say the wrong thing. Do you understand?" he asked.

She miserably nodded her head, "Yes."

As soon as Mr. Swenson's old green truck

appeared, Maggie headed for the house as ordered. She watched out the window when the men disappeared into the barn. She saw them come out again with the horses.

The men took the horses and wagon off toward the pasture with Mr. Swenson driving. They weren't gone long, but they spent lots of time outside the barn talking after that. Finally Mr. Swenson drove off, and Maggie's dad began to put the horses away.

Limping into the barn, Maggie demanded, "What happened? Did he buy them?"

"He said he had to think it over," her dad said cheerfully. "But I can tell he really wants them."

"Oh," said Maggie softly. "Then at least he won't be taking them today."

"Oh, no," said her dad. "Not until next week at the earliest."

That made Maggie feel a little better. Tim and Jamie would be out before then, she thought. She just had to have one real ride in the pasture before Molly was gone for good.

When the cousins came out Maggie had to hand it to Tim. He was one smooth operator. When Aunt Jane suggested that the three kids come berry picking, too, he was ready with some great excuses. "Oh, that would be too much walking for Maggie's ankle, and you know how whiny Jamie can get. We'd better stay here."

"I don't whine," Jamie protested. Then she caught the look Tim was giving her and added, "Well, I might get sort of cranky with all those mosquitos and sticker bushes."

"Why don't you and Aunt Betty just go by yourselves," Tim said.

His mother looked puzzled. "I thought you were the one that loved blackberries. Are you sure you want to stay here with Jamie?" she asked.

Tim nodded his head vigorously.

"But I worry about leaving you kids alone for the whole day."

"That's no problem," Maggie's mom answered. "John will be around here all day greasing machinery. He can keep an eye on them."

"Well, all right," Aunt Jane agreed. "But you kids stay close to home, do you hear?"

Three heads nodded solemnly. She didn't say how close, thought Maggie.

So the women set off for the woods loaded

down with berry buckets and looking very happy. No sooner were they out of sight when Maggie gave Tim a pat on the back. "Good work," she said happily. "Now we can get started. Just let me lock Corky in the house first."

They slipped into the barn by way of the back door. Tim took Molly's bridle, and Maggie filled her pockets with oats. She was sure her dad hadn't seen them because he was working near the machine shed.

"He'll see us if we go down the lane," Maggie pointed out. "Let's cut through the cornfield instead."

Slipping out the back door again, they crawled under the barnyard fence and into a sea of tall, green corn. No one would ever be able to find them here.

"How's your ankle?" Tim asked nervously.

"I'll be fine," Maggie assured him.

At first the horses seemed to be hiding. They weren't in the meadow or under the oak tree. They weren't in the brushy spot along the south fence row. That meant they were probably in the small trees next to the neighbor's wood lot. But where?

Suddenly Maggie stopped and stared into a thick clump of bushes. Her cousins hurried over. "What is it? Do you see the horses?" Jamie began.

"Shhh," warned Maggie. "There's a cow lying by herself in there. That could mean she's sick or something. We'd better investigate."

She crept closer with Tim right on her heels. As they approached she studied the big black and white animal. The cow was chewing her cud which told Maggie it wasn't sick.

The answer lay in the tall grass next to the cow. A second set of tiny ears flicked, and a darling little nose snuffed the cow's side. Maggie had just seen a brand new calf.

Excitedly Maggie turned to tell Tim and Jamie. Instead, her body froze. She saw Corky bounding their way barking joyfully. In a flash, she remembered other mother cows chasing after dogs. They might be in for trouble.

Sure enough, as Corky got closer, the cow lurched to its feet. Her head moved from side to side searching for the danger. She gave an angry bellow and fixed her eyes on Maggie and her surprised cousins.

"Run!" cried Maggie, giving them a push. "Run for the fence."

The three kids headed for the fence in a desperate burst of speed as Corky barked with delight. He nipped at their heels and dared the cow to catch them.

She could hear the branches breaking as the cow bolted from its hiding place. The fence wasn't far away. They just might make it.

Then Maggie fell. Her weak ankle had just buckled, and she knew she could never get up in time. The cow was coming fast. She shut her eyes and prepared to be trampled.

10

As Maggie lay helpless on the ground, she heard a thunder of hooves and an unearthly squeal. She opened her eyes to see Molly coming at full gallop with teeth bared, heading for the cow.

Before the cow could reach Maggie, Molly slammed into its side, shoving the cow away. The cow stumbled and almost went down. Then, no longer interested in charging, she hurried back to her baby.

A shudder went through Maggie's body. She felt too weak to get up. Molly was sniffing her anxiously.

"Wow," Tim exclaimed, slipping back under the fence. "I never saw anything like that before except on T.V."

"When we saw you lying there, we thought you were a goner," Jamie agreed.

Then Mr. Johnson appeared from nowhere. "What the heck do you kids think you're doing?" he panted, all winded and wild-eyed. "Don't you know that mother animals can be dangerous?"

Maggie was speechless. Where did he come from? she wondered.

Her dad gasped for breath and continued yelling at them. "I never expected anything like this. Why, if it hadn't been for Molly . . ."

"But Uncle John, how did you find us?" Tim asked.

Maggie's dad shook his head, still breathing hard. "I couldn't find you, so I let Corky out to see where he'd go," he said crossly.

"And Corky started all the trouble . . ." Maggie began.

"Oh, no," her dad interrupted. "You kids started the trouble when you went off by yourselves without telling me. I am going to give you kids such a spanking . . ."

When Maggie's mom and Aunt Jane came home, they were bewildered to find all three children standing in different corners of the kitchen with tear-stained faces.

"Mom," wailed Jamie, "it wasn't our fault." She ran to her mother crying loudly.

"What's going on here?" Maggie's mom demanded.

"Dad gave us all a spanking," Maggie sniffed, rubbing her behind.

"And he said we can't have any blackberry pie," Tim complained.

"But what did you do?" his mother wanted to know.

"I'll tell you what they did," said Maggie's dad, appearing from the living room. "They almost got themselves killed."

The women listened to his story with wide eyes, and there was complete silence after he finished. At last Aunt Jane looked at her children and said, "I can't believe you two would do such a thing!"

Maggie's mom agreed. "We specifically told you to stay close to home. Why did you want to go into the pasture anyway?"

"We were going to ride Molly," Maggie admitted, tears streaming down her face.

"Ride Molly?" gasped her mom. "All by

yourselves? Why she might have stepped on you again or worse!"

"But I've ridden her in the pasture before," Maggie mumbled. She couldn't help saying it.

"You have?" her dad asked angrily. "Then it's a good thing Molly has more sense than you do."

"Yes," Maggie's mom agreed. "And I certainly hope Mr. Swenson does take those horses away before anything else happens."

"But you can't sell Molly now," Maggie protested. "She saved my life."

"I know she did," answered her dad. "And I'll be doing her a favor to sell her to Swenson. He understands horses."

The Andersons left not long after that. "Sorry about Molly," said Tim, as he got into the car. "I guess we'll never get to ride her now."

"I'm sorry, too," Jamie agreed. "I liked her."

Maggie had orders to stay in the house while her parents brought in the new calf and its mother. But later on they agreed she could go see Molly. In the barn she offered the horse an apple and gave her a big hug.

"Thank you for being so smart and so brave," she told Molly. "I can't see why Dad still wants to sell you, but he does. I'm so sorry."

The next morning Maggie's dad got a call from Mr. Swenson saying he would buy the horses. He would be there to pick them up in an hour or so. I don't want to be around when he comes, thought Maggie, rushing to her room. I can't stand to see Molly leave. With that, the tears came, and she lay face down on her bed for a long time.

At last she heard her mom calling, "Maggie, Mr. Swenson is almost ready to leave. Don't you want to say good-bye to the horses?"

"I've got to go," Maggie said to herself, drying her eyes. "Molly is my friend. I owe her that much."

As Maggie came out the door, she saw that her dad and Polly were already going up the ramp into Mr. Swenson's truck. Mr. Swenson and Molly waited at the bottom.

"Just a minute. Wait, please," she called desperately.

The man holding Molly turned and waited. "I just have to give her one more hug," Maggie said, breathlessly throwing her arms around the horse's neck.

Maggie couldn't help crying just a little.

"Good-bye girl, and be good," she sniffled into the horse's huge shoulder. "I'll come to see you sometime."

As Molly nuzzled the girl's neck, Swenson said gently, "Don't worry. I'll take very good care of your horse, and do come see her."

"Thank you," Maggie sniffed. "I hope Dad will let me."

Then it was time for Molly to get on the truck. The men closed the door and took the ramp down. The truck pulled away leaving Maggie with a big empty spot in her heart.

She was still staring after Swenson's big truck when a little red pickup pulled into the driveway, and Mr. Green got out. "Sorry I'm late," he said. "I had to wait at a railroad crossing for a long train."

"Glad you're here," said Maggie's dad, quickly joining the man at the back of the pickup. "I'm dying to see what Maggie thinks of our replacement."

Maggie didn't move from where she stood. She couldn't figure out what they were talking about.

"Come on, Maggie," said her mom, also heading toward the pickup. "I don't think you'll be disappointed in what your dad bought this time."

And down the ramp of the little, red truck came a horse that looked very much like Molly. The color was the same, and it had the same sweet face. However, the newcomer was much smaller than Molly. It was a real live pony.

"Is she for me?" Maggie gasped. "Oh, what's her name?"

"Her name is Honey," answered Mr. Green with a big grin. "And that's just what she is, a real honey."

"Mr. Green and I went pony shopping as soon as I decided to sell the team," her dad explained. "Do you like her?"

"Oh, yes. She's beautiful, and she's just my size. I love her," Maggie bubbled. "I just wish I had an apple to give her."

"I just happen to have one handy," said her mom, handing her one.

The pony took the apple in several bites and nuzzled Maggie's shoulder, hoping for more.

"Oh, wow," said Maggie. "Wait until Kelly and the Andersons see Honey. She's the pony that I've always wanted!"